Grin and Bear It

Leo Landry

ini Charlesbridge

For Gary Poholek

First paperback edition 2014
Copyright © 2011 by Leo Landry
All rights reserved, including the right of reproduction in whole or in part in any form. Charlesbridge and colophon are registered trademarks of Charlesbridge Publishing, Inc.

Published by Charlesbridge
85 Main Street
Watertown, MA 02472
(617) 926-0329
www.charlesbridge.com

Library of Congress Cataloging-in-Publication Data
Landry, Leo.
   Grin and bear it / Leo Landry.
      p. cm.
   Summary: Will stage fright prevent a very funny bear from becoming a stand-up comedian?
   ISBN 978-1-57091-745-5 (reinforced for library use)
   ISBN 978-1-57091-746-2 (softcover)
   ISBN 978-1-60734-779-8 (ebook)
   ISBN 978-1-60734-303-5 (ebook pdf)
[1. Bears—Fiction. 2. Comedians—Fiction. 3. Stage fright—Fiction. 4. Forest animals—Fiction.] I. Title.
PZ7.L2317357Gr 2011
[E]—dc22   2010033633

Printed in China
(hc) 10 9 8 7 6 5 4 3 2 1
(sc) 10 9 8 7 6 5 4 3 2 1

Illustrations done in pencil and watercolor on Fabriano watercolor paper
Display type and text type set in Palatino Informal Sans
Color separations by Chroma Graphics, Singapore
Printed and bound February 2014 by Jade Productions in Heyuan,
   Guangdong, China
Production supervision by Brian G. Walker
Designed by Susan Mallory Sherman

Contents

-1-
A Dream

Bear had a dream. His dream was to make his friends laugh. He wanted to tell his jokes on Woodland Stage on a Saturday night. He imagined what his friends would say.

"You're so funny, Bear," Fawn would call.

"Great jokes!" Chuck would shout.

"Who knew our friend Bear was such a comedian?" Bandit would ask.

Bear had a problem, though. Whenever he spoke in front of a crowd, he got nervous. His knees knocked. His paws paused. His fur froze. He stuttered and could barely speak.

In his cozy den at home, Bear was comfortable. Each morning he wrote new jokes and practiced in front of a mirror.

"What is a bear's favorite baseball team?" he asked his reflection.

"I don't know. What *is* a bear's favorite baseball team?" Bear answered himself.

"Why, the Cubs, of course!" he replied.

"Speaking of baseball," Bear continued, "do you know the proper way to hold a bat?"

Bear paused.

"By its wings!"

After weeks of practicing, Bear was feeling more confident. He imagined his friends smiling widely. He chuckled. Perhaps this was going to be easy after all.

-2-
A Plan

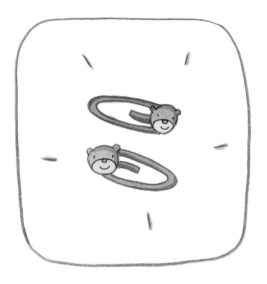

Bear woke up the next day and ate a berry breakfast. He wrote a few new jokes and practiced in the mirror.

"What do little girl cubs wear in their hair?" he asked himself.

"Bear-ettes!" he answered, snickering.

It was time to put his plan into action. Bear
grabbed his hat and went outside. He walked
through the forest to Woodland Stage.

"May I help you, Bear?" asked Tawny. "Do you need tickets for Saturday's show?"

"Yes—I mean, n-no," Bear stuttered. "I want to perform. I tell jokes," he explained to the charming fox.

"Say something funny," said Tawny.

"Um . . . ," said Bear.

"Err . . . ," mumbled Bear.

"You might want to rehearse," said Tawny. "Be here at seven o'clock sharp."

Bear's big chance had arrived. He hoped he was ready.

-3-
Ready

On Saturday Bear woke up early, feeling nervous. After breakfast he practiced in front of the mirror, as usual.

"What do you get when a bear walks through your vegetable garden?" he asked.

"Squash!" Bear replied, stomping his big bear foot in front of him.

"I think I'm getting the hang of this," he said to himself.

One by one, Bear called his friends on the telephone.

"Hi, Chuck? It's Bear. Come on down to Woodland Stage tonight. I have a surprise for you."

"Hello, Fawn? Bear here. Meet the gang at Woodland Stage at seven o'clock tonight. You'll see!"

"Everyone is going to be there, Bandit," said Bear. "Bring the whole family."

Bear hung up the telephone. He took a deep breath and let it out slowly.

"Phew! That's that," he said to himself. "Next stop, Woodland Stage!"

-4-
Showtime

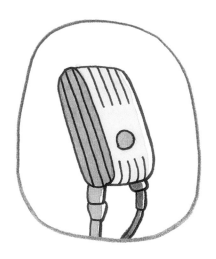

Bear arrived at the theater that evening. A large crowd had gathered. Bear checked in with Tawny at the stage door.

"There you are, Bear. Please take your place behind the curtain. The show is about to start," Tawny said. She walked onstage and began her introduction.

Yay!

"Bucks and does, pups and kits, welcome to Woodland Stage! Please put your hooves, paws, and claws together for our first performer. Here to make you laugh is Bear!" announced Tawny.

Hooray for Bear!

Go, Bear, go!

Bear parted the curtain and stepped into the spotlight. His friends hooted and hollered.

"Hooray for Bear!" shouted Fawn.

"Go, Bear, go!" cheered Chuck.

"Bear, Bear, Bear . . . ," chanted Bandit.

Bear looked out into the crowd nervously.
When he stepped up to the microphone, it happened
Again. His knees knocked. His paws paused.
His fur froze.

"What is a bear's favorite bat?" he asked the
crowd. "Wait, that's not right. . . . ," he mumbled.
He tried again.

"What do little girl cubs wear in their hair?"
he asked.

"I don't know. What *do* little girl cubs wear in their hair?" Fawn asked helpfully.

"SQUASH!" Bear answered. He stomped his big bear foot onto the stage. "Oh, wait . . . oops, wrong punch line . . ."

Bear stood there, embarrassed.

"Bear-ettes!" he shouted.

He ran off the stage into the moonlit night.

Bear ran deep into the forest.

At last he found himself at the local watering hole and went inside. Bear sat in the corner and ordered a root beer. He pulled out his list of jokes and shook his head.

"What's the use?" he asked himself. "I'll never tell another joke again." Bear crumpled up his paper full of jokes and threw it over his shoulder.

"So long, dreams," he said sadly.

Bear laid his tired head down on the table and quietly cried. Within minutes he was asleep.

-5-
Genius

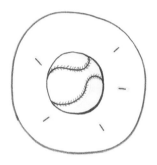

While Bear slept, a crowd gathered across the room.

"Hee hee! This is so funny! Listen to this—" A little hummingbird hovered in front of the crowd. She was reading from a crumpled sheet of paper.

"What is a bear's favorite baseball team?" she asked.

"I don't know. What *is* a bear's favorite baseball team?" yelled the crowd.

The hummingbird paused.

"The Cubs!" she chirped. "Whoever wrote this stuff is a genius," she said. "If I had jokes like this, I could really go places!"

At that moment the door burst open. Chuck, Fawn, and Bandit ran inside.

"What do you get when a bear walks through you vegetable garden?" the tiny bird asked the crowd.

"Squash!" chirped the bird, stomping her tiny foot in midair. The crowd roared with laughter.

"Wait! That's the punch line to Bear's joke!" shouted Chuck.

The forest animals turned.

"You know who wrote this?" asked the startled hummingbird. "These jokes are brilliant!"

"Our friend Bear wrote them," said Fawn. "He just performed on Woodland Stage. Well, he *tried* to perform. He ran off the stage before he finished."

"Have you seen him?" Bandit asked the crowd. "Brown bear, six feet tall, blue cap . . ."

"Nope, no bears in this crowd," answered the hummingbird. "By the way, I'm Emmy. I'd like to meet this friend of yours. May I help you look for him?"

"Sure," said Chuck, "but why do you want to meet him?"

"Well, I'm a comedian," Emmy answered. "His jokes are hilarious! Maybe he could write jokes for birds?"

-6-
A New Friend

Bear dreamed as he slept. In his dream a large crowd had gathered, and a tiny little bird was telling *his* jokes. Everyone was laughing. He could hear Chuck, Fawn, and Bandit in the crowd.

Bear smiled sleepily and began to wake up.

"Wait a minute," he said to himself. "I'm not dreaming. My friends *are* here!"

Bear walked across the crowded room.

"Hey, everyone! What are you doing here?" Bear asked.

"BEAR!" the three friends exclaimed.

Emmy darted over to introduce herself.

"You must be Bear. I'm Emmy," said the hummingbird.

Bear noticed that Emmy was carrying a crumpled
iece of paper.

"Are you picking up the trash in here?" Bear asked.

"TRASH?" twittered Emmy. "This sheet of paper is
reasure. Did you really write these jokes? Sit down.
et's talk."

Bear's friends sat down at the table.

"We've been looking everywhere for you," said Fav

"Why did you run away?" asked Chuck.

"I was nervous," Bear explained shyly. "It happens

every time. I just wanted to make my friends laugh,

that's all. Now I'll never make my dream come true."

"Are you joking?" asked Emmy. "Did you hear that pack of animals howling at your jokes? They loved them! Like I said, sit down. Bear, I think we can make both our dreams come true."

-7-
A New Dream

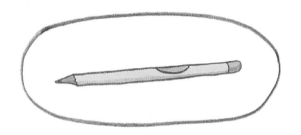

Every day for the next week, Bear woke up, put on his tie, and got to work. He sat at his desk and spent the day writing new jokes. When he was finished he tried them out in the mirror.

"What kind of bird works at a construction site?" Bear asked himself.

He paused.

"A crane!" Bear answered, chuckling.

"I have a million of them," he said to his reflection.

The next Saturday night Bear grabbed his hat and walked through the forest to Woodland Stage. He quickly headed backstage.

"Hi, Tawny," he said to the host, smiling. "It's good to be back."

"Hello, Bear," said the fox. "Hurry, the show is about to begin!" Tawny made her way onstage.

Backstage, Emmy found her friend.

"Thanks for the material, Funny Bear!" she said, giving Bear a quick kiss on the snout.

"Anytime, Tiny," said Bear, smiling.

"Bucks and does, pups and kits, welcome to this week's show. Please give a warm forest welcome to tonight's first performer—Emmy, the hilarious hummingbird!" Tawny announced.

Emmy darted onto the stage and flittered under the spotlight.

"Why do hummingbirds hum?" she chirped into the microphone.

"I don't know. Why do hummingbirds hum?" Fawn asked helpfully.

"Because we don't know the words!" cackled Emmy. The crowd went wild.

Emmy was an instant success. She took a final bow when she had finished.

"Thanks for making my night so special," she said to the crowd. "Before I go, I need to thank one more forest creature for his efforts. Let's give a big cheer for my writer—the real comedian in the room—Bear!

Tawny brought Bear onstage. He gave a little wave as he stood under the spotlight. Everyone was up on their hooves and paws, applauding.

"You're so funny, Bear," Fawn called.

"Great jokes!" Chuck shouted.

"Who knew our friend Bear was such a comedian?" Bandit asked.

Bear took a bow. He had made his friends laugh after all.